Gavin and Errol and Sophie

and Sushma and David and Kate

and Robert and Alison are . . .

...Starting School

Janet and Allan Ahlberg

VIKING

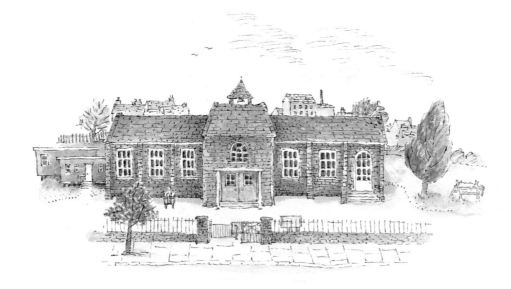

For
Val Dwelly, who gave us the idea
and
Birstall Riverside Primary School, who let us in.

VIKING

Published by the Penguin Group
Penguin Books Ltd, 27 Wrights Lane, London W8 5TZ, England
Penguin Books USA Inc., 375 Hudson Street, New York, New York 10014, USA
Penguin Books Australia Ltd, Ringwood, Victoria, Australia
Penguin Books Canada Ltd, 10 Alcorn Avenue, Toronto, Ontario, Canada M4V 3B2
Penguin Books (NZ) Ltd, 182–190 Wairau Road, Auckland 10, New Zealand

Penguin Books Ltd, Registered Offices: Harmondsworth, Middlesex, England

First published in 1988
5 7 9 10 8 6 4

Copyright © Janet and Allan Ahlberg, 1988

British Library Cataloguing in Publication Data

Ahlberg, Janet   Starting school. (Viking picture book).
I. Schools   Juvenille literature
I. Title   II. Ahlberg, Allan
371   LA132

ISBN 0-670-81688-4

Consultant Designer: Douglas Martin
Printed and bound in Great Britain by
William Clowes Limited, Beccles and London

The First Day

The children wait
in the playground

with their mums and
dads and brothers and

sisters . . . and a puppy.

The bell rings.

 Gavin and Errol

and Sophie and

Sushma  and David

and Kate and Robert and Alison

go into the school

and meet their teacher.

They hang their hats and coats in the cloakroom, have a look

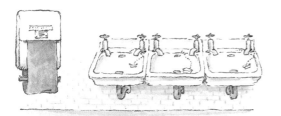

at the toilets and go into the classroom. They sit on the mat with the rest of the class.

The teacher calls the register and collects the dinner money.

She shows the children round the classroom,  and the parents too.

 In the classroom there are tables chairs and drawers for the children to keep their things in.  There is . . .

a book
corner

a home
corner

an interest
table

a box of
dressing up clothes

and a baby rabbit

in a rabbit hutch.

During the morning  Gavin

and Errol  and Sophie

and Sushma and David

and Kate

and Robert and

Alison get used to the classroom

and the rabbit gets used

to them.

At play time . . .

they go out to play.

At dinner time they eat their dinners.

In the afternoon they draw pictures,

go out to play again and have

singing in the hall.

At the end of the day they
tidy up,

have a story on the mat,

put on their hats and coats –

and go home.

The Second Day

The next day Gavin and Errol and

Sophie and Sushma and David and

Kate and Robert and Alison

go to school again.

  In the morning they do a picture and some writing in their new books.

 After that they have music and movement in the hall.

 Errol's mum plays the piano.

 At play time Robert loses
his hat ... and Alison finds it.

Errol
bangs   and the teacher
his knee,   rubs it better.

Gavin and Sushma and
David climb on the
climbing frame.

Kate <u>thinks</u> about climbing.

In the afternoon the children make
some models.

They show them to the
head teacher, have a story
on the mat and go home.

The First Week

As the days go by,

the children

get more used to the school.

On Wednesday they go into the hall
for assembly.

They listen to the
singing and say
a prayer.

They watch some older children do
a play.

On Thursday they start learning to read.

Run, run as fast as you can.

"Stop, stop little boy" Said the horse

He jumped onto the fox's back.

Gavin can read already.

He brings his book from  home to show the teacher.

Errol brings his <u>tooth</u> to show the teacher.

It came out in the night.

On Friday they go swimming in the school pool.

The water is warm and not deep. Robert  and Sushma and Kate jump up and down.

David and Sophie walk in down the steps.  Errol <u>thinks</u> about walking in.

In the afternoon Kate and Sushma and
David do cooking
with David's mum.

They make 12 little cakes,

3 big cakes

...and a mess.

Time Goes By

The next week Gavin  and

Errol and Sophie

and Sushma

and David and Kate

and

Robert and Alison . . .

choose a name for the rabbit.

They draw rabbit   pictures,

make rabbit models,

bake rabbit biscuits,

have rabbit stories on the mat, and do

lots more rabbit

things besides.

The week after that the children
have their photographs taken.

And the week after that
 Gavin loses a glove,
and Alison learns to swim;

Sophie reads  a book,

and Sushma shows her sari
and her Diva lamp.

Robert <u>thinks</u> about being in a
hallowe'en play.

And sometimes the children

are happy,

and sometimes they are sad;

sometimes puzzled – or sleepy –

or grumpy – or lumpy – or spotty!

Sometimes

the teacher is not

cheerful either.

End of Term

Christmas comes.

In the last week of term the infants

 do a play about

baby Jesus.

Everybody  has a part,

 and all the mums

and dads come

to watch.

On the last <u>day</u> of term

the children bring cakes

and crisps,

sausages,  sandwiches

and jellies, and have a party

in the classroom.

Merry Christmas Ronald

Then Gavin and Errol

and Sophie

and Sushma

and David

and Kate

and Robert and Alison

go home ...

and the holiday begins.